for Janie

Pine & Boof: Blast Off!
Copyright © 2018 by Ross Burach
All rights reserved. Manufactured in China.
No part of this book may be used or reproduced in any manner whatsoever without written
permission except in the case of brief quotations embodied in critical articles and reviews.
For information address HarperCollins Children's Books, a division of HarperCollins
Publishers, 195 Broadway, New York, NY 10007.
www.harpercollinschildrens.com

ISBN 978-0-06-241852-4

The artist used pencil and acrylic paints colored digitally to create the illustrations for this book.
Typography by Chelsea C. Donaldson
18 19 20 21 22 SCP 10 9 8 7 6 5 4 3 2 1
❖
First Edition

Pine the porcupine and Boof the bear were out collecting rocks when . . .

OOF

"What is it, Pine?"

Pine looked at the shape.
Pine looked at the color.
Pine looked at the markings.

Pine knew *exactly* what it was. . . .

"An egg . . . **FROM OUTER SPACE!**"

"It must have fallen from
a million light-years away!" said Pine.

"What do we do with it?" asked Boof.

"We have to take it back to its space nest . . . before it hatches."

"But how do we get to space?" Boof wondered.

"Easy," said Pine.

"It's not rocket science. I happen to be an expert in space travel."

But first they needed to build a rocket.

"Our spaceship's cabin!

"Rocket boosters!

"Control panels!

"I'll assemble the parts. Boof, you think of our spaceship's name."

Pine wired the control panel.

Boof tried thinking of a name.

Pine secured the rocket boosters.

Boof thought as hard as he could.

Pine affixed the wings.

Boof took a different approach.

Next, Pine quickly prepared Boof for the extremes of space travel.

Centrifuge. Check.

G-Force Launch Speed. Check.

Space Food Consumption. Check.

"Excellent technique."

"Let's take this egg home."

"Quick, Boof, into the rocket. It's time for launch."

"Yay! Lunch!" said Boof.

"No. *Launch.* We'll eat when we get there."

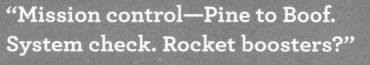

"Mission control—Pine to Boof.
System check. Rocket boosters?"

"Engaged!" said Boof.

"Fuel levels?"

"Full!"

"Sandwiches?"

"Wrapped!"

Pine set their course.

"Next stop—space."

10...

9...

8...

7...

6...

5...

4...

3...

2...

1...

down the hill.

Pine and Boof crashed to a stop, and suddenly the whole cave lit up with flickering, flapping lights.

"Pine, look."

"Stars."

"We made it to space!"

But their mission was far from over.
The two explorers set off in search
of the egg's nest.

"Look, Pine. Footprints."

Pine studied the tracks.
Pine counted the toes.
Pine measured the length.

Pine knew *exactly* what made them:

A Space MONSTER!

"Pine . . . the space egg . . . it's
HATCHING!"

But it wasn't a space monster.

. . . it was a
space *mommy*.

"We did it, Pine. We're heroes."

There was only one thing left to do. . . .

Fuel up for the long journey home.